Series 522

JESUS BY THE SEA OF GALILEE

Told by LUCY DIAMOND

Illustrated by
KENNETH INNS

Publishers: Ladybird Books Ltd . Loughborough
© Ladybird Books Ltd (formerly Wills & Hepworth Ltd) 1958
Printed in England

JESUS BY THE SEA OF GALILEE

These stories tell us about the loving work of Jesus after He began His ministry.

When He was thirty years old Jesus went from Nazareth into the wilderness of Judæa, where John the Baptist was proclaiming the coming of the promised Christ.

There John baptized Him in the river Jordan, and wondering crowds heard a Voice from Heaven saying, " This is My beloved Son."

After weeks spent alone in the wilderness, Jesus went back to Nazareth, and in the synagogue there declared that He was the One of whom ancient prophets had spoken.

Those who heard Him were angry.

" How can this man, the village carpenter, dare to say that He is the Messiah! " they cried.

In their fury they drove Him out from Nazareth.

Then Jesus went down to the Sea of Galilee and came to Capernaum, a city on the seashore.

From that day, for nearly three years, Jesus lived by the Sea of Galilee—the "Lake of Gennesaret."

What a different life from the quiet daily round of Nazareth!

The western shore of this beautiful sea was the busiest part of Galilee. The highway from Damascus through Jerusalem to the land of Egypt ran by it. The road from the famous ports of Tyre and Sidon ended there.

Capernaum, which came to be known as "His own city," was one of the busiest towns on the lake, with shipbuilding yards, fish curing sheds, and the customs offices of the Roman rulers.

People of many nations besides Jews gathered there: Greeks, Syrians, Egyptians, men from Tyre and Sidon, and Romans from the fine city which Herod had built on the seashore and named after the Roman Emperor, Tiberias.

That is why Jesus chose to begin His work—His ministry—by the sea of Galilee, where He could meet and help so many different people.

There the thing foretold by Isaiah came true:

" The land toward the sea, beyond Jordan, in Galilee of the Nations, the people which sat in darkness saw a great light."

Now the patient, loving ministry of Jesus began. He went into the synagogue in Capernaum on the Sabbath day and talked to the people. He said, " Repent, for the Kingdom of Heaven is at hand," and spoke of God their Father whom many had forgotten.

Those who heard were astonished.

" Who is this man? " they asked. " He speaks as one who has the power and authority to teach; not like the Scribes and Pharisees."

And everyone talked of this wonderful new teacher.

Jesus already had friends by the Sea of Galilee. James and John, the sons of Zebedee, a prosperous fisherman of Bethsaida, near Capernaum, were His cousins.

He also knew Andrew and Peter, two brothers who lived in Capernaum. He had met them in the wilderness of Judæa, where John the Baptist was preaching and had pointed out Jesus, saying: " Behold, the Lamb of God—the Christ." The brothers had followed Him and talked with Him for some time.

Now, walking by the sea, Jesus found Andrew and Peter and James and John busy with their work as fishermen. He called to them, " Follow Me." At once they left everything and followed Him.

Afterwards Jesus chose others to be His disciples or " learners "—a little band of twelve men who went with Him everywhere and became His dear friends.

Jesus had been teaching in the synagogue, and Andrew and Peter and James and John were with Him.

As they came out, Peter invited them all to dinner at the house where he and Andrew lived.

When they got there, Peter's wife was busy preparing a meal, but she looked sad and troubled. Peter told Jesus why his wife was so worried. Her mother was terribly ill of a fever, and there did not seem any hope that she would ever get well.

At once Jesus went to where the sick woman lay weak and helpless. He took her by the hand and raised her up.

And lo! the fever left her. She stood up strong and well, and the moment she saw that they had guests she hurried to help get the dinner ready.

What a happy gathering it was when the four disciples sat down for the first meal with their Master.

Peter's wife and her mother tried to show their thankfulness by hastening to wait on Jesus, and to offer the best of all they had to the One who had brought new life and joy into their home.

Then Peter asked Jesus if He would always stay with them when He was in Capernaum. How glad they were when Jesus said He would.

The news of this marvellous cure soon spread. As evening drew on, and the sea lay calm and still in the sunset glow, crowds came hurrying towards the house. They brought to Jesus the sick and the lame and people ill of many diseases.

And He laid His hands on them and healed them all.

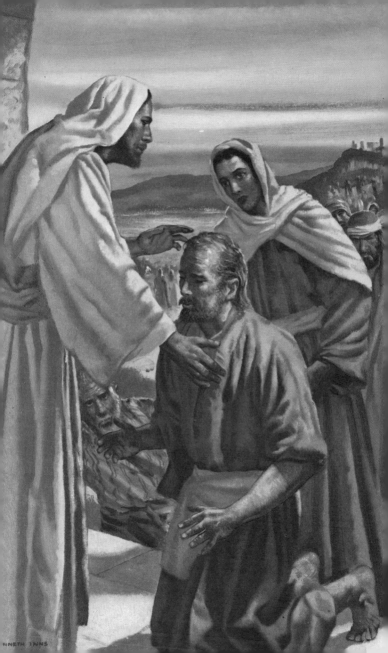

The next morning Jesus got up very early, even before it was light, and went away into a lonely place.

There, far from the town, and quite alone, He prayed.

But when it was day, crowds gathered before Peter's house and along the lakeside.

They wanted to find Jesus and hear His teaching.

But no one knew where He was.

Peter and his friends went to look for Him, and when at last they found Him, they said, " Master, everyone is seeking you. Are you not coming back? "

" No," said Jesus. " We must go into the next town along the Lake, that I may preach there also. That is why I have come."

So He led them on to Bethsaida, and afterwards to Magdala, and other villages, and in every place Jesus taught in the synagogues, and healed many.

It is lovely to think of Jesus going about Galilee as the friend of the poor, weak and helpless.

The blind and crippled came to Him for healing; and His loving hands, laid upon lepers from whom all other men shrank, brought clean new life and strength to wasted limbs.

We can picture Him on sunny days walking through the waving gold of the cornfields, or sitting on the hillside above the Lake, with His hands full of crimson and purple anemones—" lilies of the field "— the wild flowers from which He taught the people such a wonderful lesson about their Heavenly Father's love.

Jesus, however, was often to be seen on the grassy seashore in the midst of the crowd, talking to them of the things belonging to the Kingdom of Heaven.

After some time Jesus came back to Capernaum. The news soon spread that He was at home once more.

People came hurrying from all parts, and crowded into the house until there was not an inch of room even around the door.

Outside the house some men were anxiously trying to get in. They were four friends who were bringing to Jesus a man who was sick of the palsy.

The man was lying on his bed—a sort of thick padded quilt—which his friends were carrying between them.

But they could not get near Jesus for the thronging crowd.

What were they to do? They had come so far, and they could not bear to take their sick friend home again without seeing the Man who had so lovingly healed all who asked His help.

At the side of the house was a staircase leading to the flat roof.

This gave the friends an idea. They toiled up the steps, laid the sick man down, and began to uncover the roof.

When they had broken a hole large enough, they let down the bed on which the man sick of the palsy lay.

And it rested at the feet of Jesus.

The Master looked up, and saw the four friends peering eagerly through the opening to see what He would do.

He smiled kindly at these men, who had such faith in His power.

Then He spoke to the sick man: " Son, your sins are forgiven you."

Some of the Scribes were sitting near. They were very angry.

" How dare this Man speak so! " they muttered. " Who can forgive sins, but God only? "

Jesus knew their thoughts, and He turned to them.

" Which is easier to say? " He asked. " Your sins are forgiven," or to say " Arise, take up your bed and walk."

" Now you shall know that I, the Son of Man, have power on earth to forgive sins."

Then He spoke to the sick man, and clearly and triumphantly His words rang out:

" I say unto you: Arise, take up your bed and go on your way."

At once the palsied man got up, his trembling limbs steady, strong, and well. He took up his bed, looked gratefully at Jesus, and walked out before them all.

The crowd were amazed, and praised God, saying, " We never saw anything so wonderful."

How happy those friends must have felt as they all walked home along the sunny shore.

One evening Jesus said to His disciples, " Let us go over to the other side of the lake." So leaving the crowds, they began to sail across the sea.

A great storm arose. The wind, rushing between the hills, swept the water into waves like mountains, which beat over the boat until it began to sink.

But Jesus was asleep on a cushion in the stern.

The terrified disciples awoke Him. " Master, save us," they cried. " Don't you care that we perish? "

Jesus looked at them in surprise. " Why are you afraid? I am with you," He said. " Have you no faith? "

He stood up, and spoke to the wind and the sea, " Peace, be still." And there was a great calm!

Astounded and ashamed, the disciples whispered, " Who is this, that even the wind and sea obey Him? "

Jesus and His disciples spent some time on the other side, and when they sailed back to Capernaum, they found a great crowd gathered on the shore waiting for the Master.

So there was no rest for Jesus. He sat down by the sea, and patiently and lovingly began to teach, and to help those who needed Him.

Suddenly a man came rushing through the crowd and fell at the feet of Jesus. Many knew him, for he was an important person in Capernaum, Jairus, a ruler of the synagogue.

He was in terrible trouble.

"Master," he cried out imploringly, "my little daughter is dying, and she is only twelve years old. Will you come quickly to my house and lay your hands on her? I know that then she will surely be made better and live."

Jesus at once got up and followed quickly as Jairus anxiously led the way. The disciples and many others crowded after them in a great throng. They were all eager to see what would happen.

But even as they hurried on, Jesus suddenly stood still. " Who touched Me? " He asked.

Everyone waited, and no one spoke. They were all so surprised.

" But Master," Peter said, " look at the crowd pressing around. They are all so close to you, and yet you ask ' Who touched Me? ' "

" Someone did touch me," Jesus insisted. " I felt it, and I know that power has gone from Me."

There was a breathless silence—then a woman crept slowly from the crowd and knelt at the feet of Jesus. She was trembling and full of fear as she told her story.

This poor woman had been ill for years. She had been to many doctors and suffered much in the hope of being cured. Now she had spent all her money, and still was no better, but rather worse. She had heard many wonderful things about Jesus, the great Healer, and had come to find Him. As she followed among the crowd, she thought, " If I can only touch the hem of His garment I am sure I shall be cured."

So she had touched the Master's robe. At once she felt that she was better. Her painful illness was cured.

Jesus looked down very kindly at the woman crouching at His feet. His voice was very gentle, as He smiled, and said:

" Daughter, your faith has saved you and made you well. Go in peace."

As Jesus watched the grateful woman turn homewards, a messenger came running from the ruler's house.

"Don't trouble the Master any more," he said to Jairus, "your daughter is dead."

So it was all of no use !

The stricken father looked hopelessly at Jesus. The Master had overheard, and quietly comforted him.

"Fear not, only believe," He said.

He moved on quickly, and now would let none of the disciples follow Him except Peter and James and John. They came to the ruler's house, where crowds of mourners were weeping and wailing because the child had died. As He entered the door, Jesus turned to them :

"Why are you making such a noise, weeping like this ?" He asked. "The child is not dead, only sleeping."

They all laughed scornfully.

Jesus ordered them all to leave. Then, taking the sorrowing father and mother and His three disciples, He went into the quiet room where the little daughter of the house lay cold and still. Gently He lifted the child's hand and spoke to her.

" Talitha cumi," which means, " Little girl, I say unto you, Arise ! "

And her spirit heard the voice of the Master, and came back to the cold white body. The child opened her eyes, and the first thing she saw was the beautiful, kind face of Jesus looking lovingly down upon her.

He helped her from her bed, and she walked straight into the arms of her father and mother, who held her as if they would never let her go.

Could this marvellous thing really be true ?

Jairus and his wife could hardly realize
it at first. Their sorrow was turned into
unbelievable joy. The little daughter who
was dead was now given back to them
alive and well. They did not know how to
find words to thank the Master, Whose
power was so great that it was stronger and
mightier than death itself.

But Jesus understood. He always understood just how people were feeling, and
what they needed most. He turned the
mother's thoughts to the simple, homely
things of every day.

"You must give the child something to
eat," He said.

How eagerly the happy woman hurried
off to prepare a meal, a feast of rejoicing;
and one would like to think that when it
was ready, Jesus and His three disciples
would stay to share it.

As Jesus and His disciples were journeying towards Capernaum one day, the disciples were arguing among themselves. When they were back in Capernaum, they all came to Jesus, asking:

" Who is the greatest in the kingdom of Heaven ? "

Now Jesus knew that they had been disputing as to who should be first in His Kingdom. He called a child, perhaps Peter's little boy, drew him into their midst, and put His arms round him. The child looked up happily and trustfully into the face of the children's Friend.

"See this little child?" Jesus said. "I tell you, except you become as little children, you shall not enter the kingdom of Heaven."

" Whoever among you will humble himself, and will become as simple and trustful as this child, he shall be the greatest in the kingdom of Heaven."

The last time the disciples saw their Master by the Sea of Galilee was after His resurrection. The risen Lord had told them to go back to Galilee and meet Him there. So Peter and James and John, with several other disciples, were sitting on a hillside overlooking the lake, eagerly awaiting their Master. The long slow hours passed, and still Jesus did not come.

The disciples grew tired and miserable. Had their Master forgotten all about them ?

Peter looked down to where the Sea of Galilee sparkled in the evening light. That was where they had been working as fishermen when Jesus called them. Now He had not come, what could they do but go back to their old life.

Suddenly Peter got up, and turned impatiently to the others—" I'm going fishing," he said.

And just because one discouraged and hopeless man can make others feel hopeless and discouraged, too, they all said sadly :

" We will come with you."

They trailed down to the shore, launched one of the boats, and, pulling out to sea, began to cast their nets. Through the dark hours they toiled, but all that night they caught nothing. Even the old life brought failure and disappointment.

Just as the day was breaking, Jesus stood on the shore—but the weary disciples did not know that it was Jesus. Perhaps their eyes were tired with straining through the darkness. They could dimly see a figure through the morning mist, and then a Voice called across to them:

" Children, have you anything to eat ? "

Sadly they answered:

" No ! We have toiled all night, and taken nothing."

Then loud and clear came the command, " Cast the net on the right side of the boat, and you shall find."

So once more the weary disciples cast the net—and this time they could not draw it in for the weight of fish.

Ah ! now they knew. John cried joyfully, " It is the Lord ! "

When Peter heard this, he could not wait. He threw his fisher's coat around him and plunged into the sea to get more quickly to his Master.

They were near the shore, so the other disciples came in the boat, dragging the net full of fish. When they got out upon the land they saw a fire of coals, and over it a fish was cooking, and near it lay little flat loaves, all ready for a picnic breakfast on the shore.

Jesus was waiting there, and He said, "Bring some of the fish you have caught." Peter helped to draw in the net full of great fishes—one hundred and fifty-three—yet the net was not broken.

They brought some to Jesus, but not one of them had a word to say. None of them dare ask, " Who are you ? " knowing that it was the Lord. They were terribly sorry and ashamed.

They remembered other failures. All but one of them had deserted their Master in His most sorrowful hour—Peter had denied Him—yet Jesus had forgiven them. Now they had failed Him again. Their Master had come and found none of them awaiting him.

But Jesus knew how sad and tired they were. He did not reproach them—only said encouragingly " Come and have your breakfast."

It was not until they were rested and refreshed by the food they needed so badly, that Jesus turned to Peter.

" Peter," He said, " do you love me ? "

" Yes, Lord," Peter answered humbly, " you know that I love you."

" Feed my lambs," the Master told him.

Three times Jesus asked, "Do you love me ? " until Peter, almost weeping with grief and shame, cried, " Lord, you know all things ! You know that I love you."

" Feed my sheep. I leave them in your care," Jesus said, comforting him.

So by the Sea of Galilee, where they had spent many wonderful hours together, the risen Lord showed His disciples that He still trusted them.

The Good Shepherd was content to leave in their care the sheep He had loved so tenderly, and for whom He had laid down His life.

Series 522